Jessie the Lonely Puppy

Chapter One

Chloe laughed delightedly as the ducklings squabbled over the bread. It was probably a special treat for them, she decided, as it wasn't just any old bread, but the crusts of her bologna-and-cheese sandwiches. She crouched down by the edge of the lake to watch them. The ducklings polished off the last few crumbs, and then circled closer, in case she had any more. They were so sweet — mostly brown, with yellow streaks and patches, and really fluffy. Their mother was paddling watchfully around them, eyeing Chloe carefully.

A couple of the little ducks were getting braver now, swimming closer and closer. Chloe held her breath as the pair of them clambered onto the muddy edge of the lake with awkward little hops. They were coming to see her! She just wished she had some more sandwich for them. The bravest of the ducklings pecked thoughtfully at the toe of her sneaker, but didn't seem very impressed.

"Sorry," she whispered, trying not to laugh out loud and scare them away.

"I don't have anything else!"

Suddenly, there was a scuffling noise and an ear-splitting bark. A little black-and-white dog burst through a clump of reeds and nearly knocked Chloe into the lake.

The ducklings squeaked in alarm and leaped back into the water, swimming away as fast they could, little feet paddling furiously.

"Oops!" The boy chasing the dog grinned. "Sorry, Chlo. Did Jessie knock you over?"

"No, I'm just sitting in the mud because I feel like it!" she snapped. She looked out across the lake, watching the mother duck and her babies speeding off into the deeper water, away from badly behaved dogs. She wished she could swim away, too.

Jessie watched the ducklings and barked after them happily. She'd never seen ducklings before, and they were very exciting.

"Why isn't she on her leash?" Chloe asked her brother angrily, as she struggled to her feet and tried to brush the sticky mud off her jean shorts. "She's not old enough to walk on her own, Mom and Dad said. She might run off and get lost, or get into a fight with another dog."

Will shrugged. "There's no one else around, Chloe; why shouldn't she be able to run? She isn't bothering anyone."

"She's bothering me," Chloe growled. She knew she sounded grumpy and miserable, but she had really been enjoying playing with the ducks, and she'd hoped the bravest one might even have let her pet him.

Will sighed and rolled his eyes, and Jessie, bored now that the ducks had disappeared, scratched her muddy paws up against Chloe's legs, hoping for some of the bread that she could smell.

"Ow! Get her off me!" Chloe squeaked, dodging sideways and almost falling into the lake. Will grabbed her arm to pull her back, and Chloe shoved him away angrily. Jessie jumped around them with ear-splitting barks, thinking that this was all a game.

"What's going on? Are you two all right? Chloe, come away from the edge, sweetheart; you might fall in. And I'm not diving in after you!"

Chloe and Will's grandfather gently pulled them away from the water. Chloe had started crying, and Will looked angry. Jessie whined. She wasn't sure what was going on, but suddenly she didn't like this game anymore. She slunk away from the children and trotted off around the side of the lake.

"Go get her, Will," Grandpa said. "Put her back on her leash. She isn't really old enough to go off the leash yet."

Will chased after Jessie, who darted away, glad that this was a game again. Grandpa put his arm round Chloe. "What's the matter? Jessie didn't hurt you, did she?"

Chloe shook her head. "She just knocked me over and got me all muddy. But I was watching those ducks, and she chased them all away. Why does she have to be so rough?"

"She's only little, Chloe. Puppies are silly like that. And Jessie doesn't know her own strength."

Chloe sniffed and looked over at Jessie and Will, who were running back toward them now.

"Why don't you take her for a walk around the lake with Will once she's back on the leash?" Grandpa suggested gently. "I'll come, too, if you want."

Chloe hesitated. She'd like to go, if Jessie was on the leash…. But then the puppy spotted two Canada geese flying overhead and barked at full volume, jumping up and trying to catch the birds, who ignored her completely.

She shrank back against Grandpa. "No, it's okay. I'll go back and sit with Mom and Dad and read my book."

Grandpa sighed as he watched her run back to her parents, who were sitting on the picnic blanket. He followed after her slowly.

Jessie scampered off, and Will laughed as she pulled hard on her leash. She loved walks like this, with lots of different things to sniff and chase. She saw another duck in the distance and woofed happily, turning back to glance bright-eyed at Will. They raced away excitedly together.

Chloe sat down on the blanket and stared at her book, but she wasn't really reading it. It was a book about a girl and her dog, which was quite funny really, she realized. Girls who read dog books were supposed to like dogs, not be scared of them.

Chloe propped her chin on her hands and reread the first line of the page, but she just couldn't concentrate. Why hadn't she gone with Grandpa and Will to walk Jessie? She had been so excited when Mom and Dad had finally given in and said yes, they could get a puppy at last. Will and Chloe had been begging them forever. It was going to be a family dog, who belonged to everyone, even though it was Will who was the most excited. He was 10 now, and Mom and Dad had said that if he was really careful he and Chloe would be able to take the puppy out on their own, once they'd been to some dog-training classes.

Unfortunately, although the Grays had had Jessie for six weeks now and she was old enough to go out for walks, the dog-training classes had been at the same time as Will's football practice, so Jessie hadn't been to any yet. Will didn't mind too much. He and Dad took her for really long walks when Dad got home from work, or sometimes he went with Grandpa.

But Chloe didn't go at all. She had been sure that everything would be okay.

She couldn't possibly be scared of a tiny little puppy, could she? When they'd had a family discussion to decide what kind of dog they should get, she had said she didn't mind as long as it was friendly and sweet, and not too big. And not a boxer.

It had been a boxer who'd frightened her three years ago, back in her first year at school. She'd been running after Mom and Will through the park on the way home, and she'd gotten a little too close to the big dog. It had thought she was going to snatch the stick it was playing with and snapped at her. The boxer hadn't really hurt Chloe, just torn her sweater sleeve, but she had been terrified, and Mom had been furious with the dog's owner.

She'd told the boy that his dog should be on a leash if it wasn't properly under control. She'd said she'd report him to the police if she ever saw it loose in the park again.

Then Mom had explained to Will and Chloe that they mustn't ever, ever go near strange dogs, even if they looked friendly. Chloe had known that already, of course, but she hadn't meant to upset the dog. She'd just run a little too close.

For a while after that, she would beg Mom to take them the long way home from school so they didn't have to go through the park, where there were always people walking dogs. But that had been three years ago. She could walk through the park now, although she wouldn't pet even the friendliest dogs.

Chloe had been certain that a puppy would be all right. She loved the *idea* of having a dog, and a puppy that she knew from when it was tiny — surely she wouldn't be scared….

But it hadn't worked out like that at all. The first time Chloe had seen Jessie, the Border Collie puppy was beautiful — so fluffy, like a little black-and-white ball. They had gone to see the litter of puppies at the breeder's, and Chloe and Will had laughed at the funny little puppies climbing over each other and bouncing around their cage. Chloe had been so excited, and when she finally found the courage to pet the little black-and-white head, Jessie had licked her hand with a tiny pink tongue. Chloe had loved her right away.

She could see Will and Jessie now, playing by the tall trees at the edge of the lake, Jessie jumping excitedly at the stick that Will was waving. It was the kind of energetic game Jessie loved.

That was Chloe's problem. Jessie wasn't just fluffy and sweet. She was jumpy, too, and wriggly and loud. Will played with her all the time, and that made her even more excited. She would jump around his feet, barking away, and Chloe couldn't help looking at her sharp little white teeth. She'd been looking forward to the puppy curling up on her lap for a cuddle sometimes, but Jessie just didn't seem to be that kind of dog.

Chloe tried to hide it, but even though she wanted to, she was too scared to touch her. And Jessie had Will, who loved her so much. Why would she bother with a girl who never petted her, and pulled away even if Jessie just gave her an interested sniff?

Chapter Two

Chloe was half-reading, half-listening to Grandpa and her parents chatting when a loud bark made her jump. She watched as the puppy suddenly appeared from among the trees, streaking toward them in a black-and-white blur.

"She's running around off her leash again," she said nervously.

Mom looked at Jessie. "She's just having fun, Chloe. Don't worry."

Jessie stopped a little ways away from the picnic blanket and barked again anxiously. She needed them to come now, but they were just staring at her. She pawed at Chloe's leg, but Chloe pulled away with a frightened squeak.

Jessie shook her ears. Why did Chloe always do that? Frantically, she ran back toward the trees a little ways and barked again.

"I think something's wrong," Dad said, frowning and getting up. "Where's Will?"

Will! Yes, they'd understood at last! Jessie whined again, and then wagged her tail as Dad and Chloe finally followed her. Will had told her to go and get them, and even though she hadn't wanted to leave him, she was desperate to help.

"Oh, no…," Dad muttered as they got closer to the trees. Huddled at the bottom of one of the taller trees was Will. Dad and Chloe broke into a run.

"It's all right, we're here now," Dad said, as he crouched by Will.

"I fell — I got really high up and a branch broke…," Will said faintly.

"Don't worry. Everything will be okay," Dad said soothingly. He turned to Chloe. "Go get your mom and tell her to call an ambulance. I think Will might have broken his leg."

Jessie sat in the kitchen in her basket, whimpering every so often. She didn't know what was happening, but things were definitely not right. And she didn't know where Will was.

"Shh, shh, Jessie," Grandpa said gently, stroking her head. "Don't worry. Poor Jessie. It must have been very scary for her, seeing Will like that."

"It was scary for everyone," Chloe whispered, cupping her hands around her hot chocolate. Grandpa had made it for her. He said even though it was summer, there was nothing like hot chocolate when people were upset. But it didn't seem to be working.

"I wish Mom would call." Chloe stared hopefully at the phone, as though that would make it burst into life. "She promised she'd call as soon as she had some news."

Grandpa patted Chloe's hand, a bit like he'd petted Jessie. "I know it was scary, but Will's going to be well taken care of. A broken leg heals quickly, and Will is healthy and strong. He was awake and talking to us, and that's the important thing."

Chloe nodded. She supposed her grandpa was right, but Will's leg had been all twisted and awful-looking.

At last the phone rang, and Chloe spilled her drink all over the table.

Grandpa reached for the phone before Chloe could grab it. "Hello, honey. What's happening?"

Chloe hovered next to Grandpa, trying to hear, but it was mostly just *Mm-hm* and *Right*, from his end. She couldn't hear what Mom was saying.

Finally, Grandpa put down the phone.

"Didn't she want to talk to me?" Chloe asked, sounding hurt.

"She didn't have long, Chlo. Will's going to have an operation on his leg. She needed to be with him."

Chloe stared at him. "An operation? But I thought he'd just have a cast put on it! Isn't that what you do for broken legs? That's what Maddie had when she broke her arm."

Grandpa nodded. "It's a pretty bad break — he fell a long way. He's going to have some special pins put in his leg to hold the bone while it heals."

"Is Will going to have to stay in the hospital for long?" Chloe asked, tracing patterns in hot chocolate on the plastic tablecloth. She'd wiped it up, but not very well.

Jessie came and stood with her paws on Grandpa's knee. She could hear them talking about Will. Where was he? When was he coming home?

"For a while," Grandpa replied. "Mom wasn't sure. I'm going to stay here for a couple of nights to take care of you."

Chloe felt her throat tighten. She had thought Will would be home tonight. Staying in the hospital sounded scary.

Jessie looked at Chloe. Was she worried about Will? What was going on? She whimpered, staring up at Chloe and Grandpa hopefully. But Chloe just turned away and walked quickly out of the room, her eyes filling with tears.

"Let's leave her alone to calm down," Grandpa said to Jessie.

Jessie stared up at him with big, sad eyes. Everyone was upset, and the house felt strange without Will. She wanted him to come home and play fetch with her in the yard.

Grandpa sighed and tickled her behind the ears. "I know, Jessie. I want

28

him home, too. But it's going to be just us for a while."

The last week of school before summer vacation was usually so much fun. But this year, everything seemed different. Will and Chloe usually walked to school together, because it was only around the corner, and Will was in middle school and old enough to be responsible, Mom said. But all that week, Chloe had to walk to school with Grandpa, because she couldn't go by herself. Jessie came, too, because Grandpa said she really needed some exercise.

Chloe missed Will, and Mom and

Dad, too. They were spending a lot of time at the hospital with Will, and Grandpa was going to stay at Chloe's house for the rest of the week to help. She loved Grandpa, but she couldn't help feeling a little left out. At least she had horse camp to look forward to. She and her friend Maddie were spending the second week of the vacation staying at a ranch, where they'd each get to take care of their own special pony all week. They were going horseback riding, and they'd be learning to jump, too. Chloe couldn't wait.

Maddie met them halfway to school as usual. She knew all about Chloe's issues with Jessie, but she loved dogs, too.

"She's so pretty," Maddie told Chloe,

as Jessie trotted alongside them. "I know what you mean about her being energetic, but she's so cute!"

Chloe sighed. Even though Maddie was her best friend, and she was trying really hard to understand how Chloe felt about Jessie, she just couldn't. Maddie loved dogs almost as much as Will!

On Tuesday after school, Mom picked Chloe up in the car to take her to visit Will. She'd seen him for five minutes the day before, but he'd still been sleepy after the operation, and she wasn't sure he'd really known she was there. Chloe was desperate to see him, but a little nervous at the same time. She knew he was going to ask about Jessie, and she didn't know what to say.

Chloe was starting to worry about the puppy. She spent most of her time moping in her basket, or perched on the window seat in the living room, where she usually sat to watch for Will walking home from school. Obviously she was waiting for him to come, and whenever she heard Mom or Dad pulling up in the car, she would rush to the door barking excitedly, her tail wagging. Then as soon as she realized Will wasn't with them, she would slink sadly back to her basket.

Will had a big cast on his leg, but otherwise he was his old self. Except that he hated having to keep still.

Chloe perched on the edge of Will's bed, while Mom went over to speak to one of the nurses.

"I can't believe I'm going to be stuck in bed forever!" he groaned.

"Does it hurt?" Chloe asked, biting her lip.

"No, it's all right. I've got medicine to stop it from hurting. It's itchy, though." Will frowned. "Chloe, how's Jessie? Is she missing me? Mom says she's fine, but I think she's just saying anything to make me feel better."

Chloe glanced over at Mom, who was still talking to the nurse. She knew what he meant. But she didn't want to upset Will, either. Worrying about Jessie would only make him feel worse.

"She's okay," Chloe said carefully. "She does miss you, but Grandpa's taking her for walks, and she comes with us to school and back."

"But Grandpa can't run, Chloe. He's too old! Jessie needs a lot of exercise. And I was supposed to take her to dog-training during summer vacation." He looked worried. "Couldn't you go for walks with Grandpa?" Will pleaded. "I know you're nervous with Jessie, but if Grandpa was there, too…."

Chloe looked at her fingers. "We all walk to school together," she repeated. But she knew that wasn't really what Will meant.

"Come on, Chloe. Will needs to rest now. You can come back and see him soon." Mom had finished talking, and was looking at Will's pale face with concern.

Chloe hardly spoke on the way home, until they were just turning onto their street. "How long is Will going to be there?" she asked suddenly.

"I'm really not sure, Chloe," Mom answered. "He should have been able to come home soon after the operation, but the nurse said they're a little worried that the bone pieces haven't fit back together correctly yet. It could be a while — a few weeks, even."

"Weeks?" Chloe whispered in horror. She hadn't thought it could possibly be that long. She would miss his silly jokes. And Jessie would be heartbroken.

The puppy was waiting hopefully by the door when they got home, and her drooping ears made Chloe feel so guilty. She'd said to Will that Jessie was okay, but now she looked so miserable. Chloe sighed. If she'd told Will that, it would have made him miserable, too. There was nothing he could do about it, stuck in the hospital.

But I could help, Chloe told herself. *I could try and cheer Jessie up.*

She followed Jessie into the kitchen, and watched as she slumped down into her basket. Chloe felt so sorry for her, sitting there with her head hanging.

"Hey, Jessie," she said gently, crouching by the basket.

Jessie ignored her. She wanted Will, and he still hadn't come back to her. She didn't like it when he went to school every day, but at least he always came home. Where was he now? And why hadn't he taken her with him?

Chloe nervously darted out a hand to pat Jessie, but she patted her too hard, and when Jessie wasn't expecting it.

Jessie was feeling so upset that when Chloe touched her, she jumped around and barked sharply, showing her teeth. What was going on? She stared angrily at Chloe, who was scrambling away, crying. Silly girl!

Why couldn't Chloe just leave her alone?

Chapter Three

Chloe kept away from Jessie after that. Her behavior had brought back all those bad memories of the dog in the park. Chloe visited Will, and spoke to him on the phone a couple of times, but whenever he asked her about Jessie, she just said that Grandpa was taking her for lots of walks and wriggled out of saying more than that.

Grandpa really loved dogs, and Jessie liked him, but it wasn't the same as racing all over the park with Will. The puppy was bursting with energy, and a couple of short walks a day just weren't enough. Jessie was used to a quick walk before school, and then another really long one with Will and Dad later on. But Dad was working late so he could fit in visiting Will in the hospital. He didn't have much time for dog-walking. Collies needed a lot of exercise, and Jessie really hated being stuck in the house. She was bored.

It was the first morning of vacation, so Jessie hadn't even had her walk to school. She wandered around the house with her leash, looking hopeful, but Mom was busy picking out some books to take to Will, and Jessie knew Chloe wouldn't take her. Mom had encouraged Jessie to go out into the yard, but that was no fun without someone to play with. She looked around the kitchen, trying to find something interesting to do. She pushed her squeaky bone across the floor for a while, but what she really needed was for Will to throw it for her to chase.

Her bone was up against the kitchen cupboards now, so Jessie scratched with one paw to get it back into the middle of the floor. But her claws caught on the cupboard door instead. It opened a little ways, and then banged shut.

Jessie stared at it, fascinated. Then she carefully hooked her claws around the edge of the door again. Once more, the door bounced and banged.

The next time, she pulled it a little too hard, and it didn't bang back. Jessie went to nudge the door again with her nose, but then she caught a delicious and interesting smell coming from the cupboard.

There was food in there. Jessie used her nose to push the door open a little more and found the cereal boxes.

"Oh, no! Mo-om!" Chloe was standing in the kitchen doorway, staring at Jessie, who looked back rather guiltily. She was surrounded by chewed-up cardboard and an awful lot of cornflakes.

"What's the matter? Oh, Jessie!"
Mom had come downstairs and was
staring at the mess in horror. "You bad
dog!" she said angrily. "What a waste. I
hope you're not going to be sick now."

Jessie flattened herself on the floor
and whined miserably, backing toward
her basket. She hadn't meant to be bad.
The cereal had smelled so good, and the
cardboard boxes had been fun to tear up
with her teeth….

Mom sighed. "Oh, Jessie. It isn't really your fault. You need a walk, don't you?"

Jessie thumped her tail on the floor, just once, but she stayed down, watching Mom clean up the mess. She *was* sorry, but she still felt grumpy and bored. She desperately wanted something to do.

Chloe helped her mom clean up. When they finished, Mom gave her a hug. "Not the best way to spend the first day of vacation, is it? Should we go out for ice cream together after we've been to see Will this afternoon? I feel like I've hardly seen you recently."

Chloe hugged her back, almost spilling a dustpan full of cornflakes. "Yes, please! Thanks, Mom!" She danced over to empty the cornflakes in the garbage can. "Don't worry about having to go to the hospital so much. I'll be at horse camp next week with Maddie, so you won't need to worry about me then."

She turned around smiling, but then her eyes widened as she saw her mother's face. "What is it?"

"Oh, Chloe! I never called them! It was one of my jobs for the day after Will had his accident, and I never called them to sign you up!" Mom looked horrified. "Where's the brochure? I'll call them now."

She grabbed the phone, and Chloe watched her making the call. Her mom frowned a little as she explained, and then looked terribly disappointed and guilty. Chloe knew what Mom was going to say before she even put down the phone.

"I'm so sorry. They're all booked up. They've promised to call me if there's a cancellation, but they didn't sound very hopeful. Oh, Chlo, I feel awful…."

Chloe stared at the ground. She wanted to say it was okay; she knew Mom had had other things on her mind. But she had been looking forward to this for so long! She and Maddie had spent hours at school talking about it, and drawing pictures of the ponies they might get to take care of. How was she going to tell Maddie? It would ruin her vacation, too!

She swallowed hard, trying not to yell at Mom. She knew she hadn't done it on purpose. But it was so unfair!

She dashed out of the kitchen,

scrambled up the stairs to her room, and flung herself onto her bed, crying. Mom spent all this time worrying about Will, and she'd just forgotten about her. She mattered too, didn't she?

She cried so much that her head hurt, and then she actually fell asleep, in the middle of the day.

Mom came in just after she'd woken up, which made Chloe think she'd probably been hanging around outside her room for a while. She had a plate with a sandwich and some cookies on it.

"You missed lunch," she said gently. "Bologna and cheese." It was Chloe's favorite. She wiped her eyes and took the plate gratefully.

"I spoke to Maddie's mom and

explained. I said I'd arrange something really special for you girls later in the vacation."

Chloe just nodded.

"I really am sorry, Chlo."

She looked sorry, and Chloe leaned against her shoulder. Crying made her feel awful, and she felt guilty now, too. At least she wasn't stuck in the hospital like Will. "I know," she muttered.

"Are you still coming with me to visit Will tonight?" Mom asked. "I know he's looking forward to seeing you. He asked if you could bring him some video games."

Chloe nodded. "Mmm. I know which ones he likes. I'll find them after I've eaten this."

"Thanks, Chlo. You're wonderful." Mom kissed the top of her head and went back downstairs.

Chloe didn't feel wonderful. She felt lonely and miserable. She ate the cookies, but she didn't really enjoy them, and then she got up to go and get Will's video games from his bedroom.

She was searching through the pile on his shelf when a tiny noise made her turn around sharply.

She hadn't noticed that Jessie was lying on Will's bed, staring at her, her eyes looking even darker than usual and so sad. For once, Chloe didn't feel that horrible wave of fright that she got when a dog was too close. Jessie just seemed so unhappy.

"You look like I feel…," Chloe joked, but it wasn't really funny. "Mom isn't angry with you anymore, Jessie, honestly."

Jessie gazed at Chloe and thought she looked sad, too. She whined, and Chloe nodded.

"I know. You miss Will, don't you?" Chloe picked up the games, then wriggled herself over to lean against Will's bed. "Me too, Jessie."

Jessie gave a huge sigh, and Chloe giggled. "That was right in my ear."

She looked at Jessie, whose nose was hanging over the edge of the bed right next to her, and very gently petted her.

Jessie closed her eyes and sighed again, gratefully, as Chloe scratched behind her ears. It felt so nice to have somebody pay attention to her.

Chloe lay in bed that night feeling too hot to sleep. Mom had said she thought it might thunder, but even though a storm would probably cool everything down, Chloe hoped she was wrong. She hated thunderstorms. She turned over and yawned. She was tired, but she was never going to be able to sleep in this sticky room….

She was woken hours later by a huge crash of thunder. Her room was still lit up by lightning, which meant the storm was right overhead. Chloe sat up, clutching the comforter around her shoulders. Another flash! The horrible blue-white light sent everything into scary shadows, and she shivered, waiting for the thunder.

Suddenly, a little black-and-white body hurtled through her bedroom door, making Chloe squeak with surprise. Jessie flung herself onto Chloe's bed, whimpering in fear.

"Oh, Jessie, are you scared of thunder, too?" Chloe cuddled the puppy close, forgetting to be frightened, either of Jessie or the thunder. As the next thunderclap cracked overhead, Jessie cowered against her, letting Chloe wrap her arms around her small black ears to shut out the noise. "Ssshh, ssshh, it's okay. It'll go away soon."

Jessie licked her hand gratefully. She couldn't have stayed in the kitchen, not with those crashing noises and that awful prickly feel in the air. She really wanted Will, but Chloe would do. It was nice to be cuddled, and she was making good sounds, shushing noises that made the crashing seem not so bad.

She could feel Chloe's heart thudding so quickly. *She's scared too*, Jessie thought. She licked her again, and then snuggled closer as another crash of thunder rumbled around the house.

Chloe lie there, jumping every so often as the thunder rang out, but mostly thinking over and over, *I'm cuddling Jessie. I'm holding a dog! I'd never have thought that she'd be scared of thunder, when she's so bouncy and loud.* "You're even worse than me, Jessie." She giggled, and Jessie licked her under the chin.

The thunder was dying away now, to just a few grumbles, and Chloe lay back down, with Jessie still cuddled up next to her. "Are you staying, Jessie?" she asked.

But Jessie was asleep already, curled in a little ball in the crook of Chloe's arm.

Chapter Four

Jessie was still there when Chloe woke up the next morning, snuggled on the side of her bed. Chloe smiled delightedly — it was just like she'd imagined having a dog would be. Jessie yawned, showing a huge length of pink tongue, and rolled over onto her back, still fast asleep. She lay there with her paws folded on her chest, snoring a little, until Chloe woke her up by giggling too much.

"Sorry, Jessie. You looked so funny."

Jessie let out another enormous yawn, then gave Chloe a big face-washing lick.

"Ugh! Now I'm really awake." Chloe got out of bed and followed Jessie downstairs to the kitchen, where Mom was making toast.

"I was wondering where Jessie had gone!" Mom said, looking slightly surprised. "You slept late! I was just about to come and wake you up. It's vacation club this morning, remember?"

Chloe nodded. Her mom worked part-time at the library, so in the mornings she and Will usually went to a vacation club at one of the schools nearby. Even though she didn't usually hang around with Will — he stuck with the boys, mostly — it would feel weird being there without him.

Jessie watched sadly through the front window as they got into the car without her. She'd been hoping for a walk. She had that itchy, bored feeling again. She trotted back into the kitchen and out into the yard through her dog door. She sniffed around for a while and snapped at a few butterflies, then she just lay on her side in a sunny patch, flicking her tail idly.

A beetle wandered past her nose, and Jessie rolled over to stare at it as it ambled off between her paws. She crept after it, tail wagging slightly, and watched it climb under some stones in the flowerbed. Where did it go?

Jessie pawed at the stones, but the beetle was gone. She scratched some more, then dug furiously, her paws spraying up stones and dirt. The beetle was long gone, but the digging was fun. Jessie happily clawed and scraped and scratched, loving the exercise.

Then she fell asleep, her nose in a pile of dirt, worn out and snoozing blissfully.

"Jessie!"

Jessie sat up with a jump, blinking sleepily, and saw that Chloe was there, looking down at her with her hands over her mouth.

"Oh, Jessie, Mom's going to be so annoyed. Dad gave her that plant for her birthday." Chloe quickly grabbed a trowel from the shed to scoop some of the earth back into the flowerbed. "We have to clean up. Maybe she won't notice."

But it was too late. Chloe's mom was standing by the back door, looking horrified. In fact, she looked more than horrified. She looked furious.

"You bad dog! Look at this mess! Oh, I don't believe it! My beautiful camellia…." She crouched to look at the plants that Jessie had uprooted.

Jessie hung her head sadly. She'd only been playing….

"I think she was bored, Mom," Chloe said quickly. "Please don't be angry with her. She misses Will, and all the walks he and Dad used to take her on. And now that Grandpa's not staying anymore, she's hardly getting any exercise at all."

Chloe petted Jessie, feeling her shiver. It was obvious that she hated being shouted at. Chloe frowned. "Mom, could Maddie and I take Jessie for a walk? Just to the park. We could run around with her and work off some of her energy; I'm sure she wouldn't be so naughty then."

Mom shook her head. "You're not old enough, Chlo. And I thought you were terrified of dogs! And Jessie is such a handful. But you're right, she does need more exercise."

Chloe helped her try to fill in the dirt around the camellia again. "Mom, you let Will walk me to school all last year, and he's only a year older than me. And I'll be with Maddie, too! She'll help me with Jessie. We'll be fine!"

Her mom sighed. "Well, it might be worth a try. I'm sure she's only being naughty because we're not spending enough time with her."

Chloe threw her arms around Mom. "Thank you! I'll go call Maddie!"

"This is great, Chloe. I can't believe you aren't scared of Jessie anymore." Maddie was looking admiringly at Chloe walking with Jessie on her leash.

Chloe smiled. "I can't, either. But it's wonderful."

Jessie was scampering along happily, sniffing the interesting smells and hoping they were going to the park so she could run really fast, like she did with Will. She still wished he would come back, but Chloe was her person now, too. Chloe had taken care of her during that horrible, scary night, and that made her special.

They raced all over the park for an hour, until the girls were exhausted, although Jessie was still bright and bouncy.

"She's not tired at all!" Maddie panted, collapsing on a bench. "Look at her. She wants to run again!"

Jessie barked excitedly. She could see

a squirrel scurrying along between those trees, and she loved chasing squirrels. She looked up hopefully at Chloe and tugged on the leash.

"I'm sorry, Jessie, but we've got to get home. I promised Mom we'd be back by five." Chloe turned to walk Jessie out of the park, and Jessie gave the squirrel a last longing look and followed her.

But then the squirrel changed direction and started to run along the grass almost in front of Jessie's nose. It was too much to bear. She gave an enormous bark and flung herself after the squirrel.

Chloe gasped as she felt the leash almost pulling out of her hand. "Hey! Jessie, no! Come back!"

Jessie was so strong. Chloe tried desperately to get her under control, but she was only just managing to hold on as Jessie dragged her after the squirrel. They galloped over the grass, and then Jessie cut across one of the paved paths that ran through the park. Chloe tripped on the edge of the grass and went flying, finally letting go of the leash.

Jessie sped up. She was going to catch a squirrel at last! But the squirrel had made it to the trees, and all Jessie could do was bark angrily at it as it disappeared into the leafy branches. Disappointed, she turned to go back to Chloe.

Chloe! There she was, lying on the path. She was crying! Jessie let out a terrified whimper and raced over, throwing herself onto the ground next to Chloe and whining miserably.

Chloe had scraped her knee on the pavement, and blood was dripping down her leg. Maddie was trying to wipe it with a tissue, but it was a nasty cut.

"Oh, Jessie, it's okay." Chloe sniffed. "Don't be upset." She could see why Jessie was frightened, and she felt so sorry for her. Will had been hurt, and he'd gone away. Now Jessie thought that Chloe was going away, too.

"Are you all right to walk?" Maddie asked, helping Chloe to her feet.

"I'm fine," Chloe said. "Let's go home."

Maddie took Jessie by the leash. "Just don't go too fast, Jessie, okay?"

They slowly made their way back, with Chloe leaning on Maddie and Jessie trotting obediently alongside her.

Chloe's mom was watching for them through the front window. She looked worried.

"Are we really late?" Chloe muttered.

Maddie frowned. "A little. And she wasn't sure about letting us go, was she?"

Mom flung open the front door. "Chloe, you promised me five— Oh, no, what did you do?" She helped Chloe inside, and Jessie and Maddie crept in behind them, not wanting to be noticed.

"What happened?" Mom asked, taking down the first-aid box. She looked very upset — much more upset than she ought to be about just a scraped knee, Chloe thought.

"Jessie ran after a squirrel and I tripped," she explained, trying not to make it sound too serious.

"That dog again!" Mom said angrily.

"She didn't mean to hurt me! She was really sorry — she was whimpering," Chloe protested. But she could see that Mom wasn't really listening.

"She's too willful. I don't know what we're going to do with her," Mom said, dabbing at Chloe's knee with a tissue.

"Oh, she isn't really, Mom!" Chloe
protested, giving Maddie a horrified
look. "She's wonderful! She didn't mean
to hurt me."

Jessie sat in her basket, her eyes
swiveling between Mom and Chloe,
shivering at the loud, upset voices.
Mom kept looking at her as though
this was all her fault. And Jessie had a
horrible feeling that it was.

Chapter Five

Will smiled and shook his head as he spotted Chloe walking up the hallway, a big bandage on her knee. "I know you miss me, Chlo, but cutting your leg off so you can stay in the hospital, too, that's just not smart.... Seriously, what did you do?"

Chloe grinned at him. "I took Jessie for a walk! Well, Maddie and I did."

She looked down at the bandage and shrugged. "But Jessie wanted to chase a squirrel, and I tripped…."

Will beamed. "That's great!"

"Hey!"

"Not your knee! Great that you took Jessie out. Thanks, Chlo. I'd been really worrying about her."

Chloe sighed and glanced over at her mom, who was talking to the doctor. "I'm not sure Mom's going to let me take her out again, though," she whispered. "She was so angry. Jessie has been really naughty the last couple of days."

Will thought for a moment. "Well, if you really can't talk Mom into it, maybe you can wear off some of her energy in the yard. She loves playing fetch, and you could try hiding one of her toys and getting her to play hide-and-seek. Then maybe Mom will be a little less mad."

Chloe nodded. "Good idea. Anyway, I might still get Mom to give in."

"You just need to stretch your legs, don't you, Jessie?" Chloe said, petting Jessie's silky black-and-white back, as they leaned against the sofa watching TV.

Jessie let out a huge sigh, as if in agreement, then slumped down with her head in Chloe's lap.

Chloe had spent a long time trying to convince her mom that Jessie had only tripped her up by accident. But Mom was still saying that she didn't think it was a good idea for Chloe and Maddie to take Jessie out again. Chloe was also worried about what her mom had said about not knowing what to do with Jessie. What did that mean? She was scared that her mom might want to send Jessie back to the breeder they'd gotten her from. Will would be heartbroken.

And it wasn't just Will. Chloe would miss Jessie so much, too, she realized now. She was determined to turn Jessie into the most perfect dog ever, so Mom wouldn't want to get rid of her. But that meant they had to go out for more walks. Chloe was sure that Jessie was only acting up because she needed a lot more exercise, and the occasional short walks she was getting with Grandpa just weren't enough. Chloe had spent the morning playing in the yard with Jessie, like Will had suggested, but she was sure that Jessie really wanted more space for a good long run.

Eventually, after an entire day of begging, Mom agreed to let Chloe and Maddie take Jessie out. But she made Chloe take her cell phone so they could call home if anything went wrong.

Luckily, Jessie seemed to know that she had to be on her best behavior. She walked quietly all the way to the park, trotting along next to Chloe. Chloe and Maddie smiled at each other as a couple of elderly ladies commented on what a well-behaved dog Jessie was.

"I wish we could get them to say that to my mom!" Chloe whispered, and Maddie giggled.

Chloe's leg was still a little too sore for her to run really fast, so Maddie took Jessie's leash when they got to the park.

Jessie looked up at Maddie and Chloe, her ears pricked, but she didn't race off.

"What's up, Jessie?" Maddie asked her gently.

Chloe leaned down to pet her, and Jessie nuzzled her gently, pressing her cool, damp nose into Chloe's hand. Chloe rubbed Jessie's ears. "It's okay, Jessie. You go! Run with Maddie!"

"But not too fast!" Maddie added, smiling.

Jessie wagged her tail delightedly, swishing it like a flag, and sprinted away, but she kept coming back to check on Chloe, who was sitting on one of the benches.

"She's really worried about you," Maddie said, panting. Jessie had just raced to the other side of the trees and back. "She's such a sweetheart."

Jessie sat on the path, laid her muzzle on Chloe's lap, and stared up at Chloe anxiously. Was Chloe all right? Jessie swept her tail back and forth across the path when Chloe beamed at her.

Maddie flopped onto the bench, too. "We should head back, shouldn't we?" she asked, checking her watch.

Chloe nodded. "Let's go home past the shops to give Jessie a change of scenery," she suggested. She took the leash from Maddie and got to her feet.

Jessie looked up at them both, and her tail stopped wagging. Home? Already? But she wanted to run some more! That had hardly felt like a walk at all.

"Do you think your mom will let you

take Jessie out on your own next week, when I'm at horse camp?" Maddie asked, as they walked through the park gates.

Chloe frowned. She hadn't really thought about that. "I haven't mentioned it yet, but I can't see her saying yes. She'd be too worried that something might happen to us. Maybe I can ask Grandpa to come with me…."

"Do you mind if I stop in and buy a magazine?" Maddie asked, as they went past the corner store.

Chloe shook her head. "Of course not. We'll wait for you outside. Sit, Jessie!"

Jessie looked at Chloe doubtfully, and Chloe gently pushed her to sit down. She'd been reading on the Internet about dog-training, and she'd tried practicing with Jessie in the yard, but they weren't very good at it yet. Eventually Jessie sat, and Chloe praised her lovingly.

Maddie took forever. Chloe could see her through the window, trying to decide which magazine to buy.

Chloe gazed down at her feet, thinking sadly about horse camp and how cool it would have been. But then, if she'd gone Jessie would have been really lonely without her, she supposed. Maybe it was all for the best.

Jessie soon got bored of sitting still and watching people going in and out of the store. Lots of them had interesting things in their bags, though. She sniffed hopefully. Delicious-smelling things.

Suddenly, Jessie pulled sharply at her leash, and Chloe gasped as she dragged it out of her hand. Before Chloe could catch her, Jessie was right outside the store's front door, digging in a big shopping bag that a lady had put down while she found her car keys.

"Jessie, no!" Chloe squeaked, horrified, as the lady tried to pull her bag away.

"Is this your dog?" she demanded furiously. "What on earth were you doing, letting go of her like that?"

"I'm really sorry!" Chloe said, blushing scarlet. "Oh, Jessie...." She finally managed to grab Jessie's leash and pull her out of the shopping bag, but it was too late. She had a cookie in her mouth, and there was a package sticking out of the bag, ripped open by her sharp little teeth.

"She's eating my cookies!" the lady shouted. She looked so angry that Chloe thought she might explode.

"I'm so sorry. I'll pay for them," she gasped, frantically digging in her skirt pocket for her money, while trying to

81

hold onto Jessie's collar with her other hand.

Jessie had finished the delicious cookie, but she was beginning to realize that she'd done something wrong. The lady with the bag was shouting at Chloe. Jessie squirmed behind Chloe's legs to hide.

Chloe quickly pressed a couple of dollar bills into the lady's hand, muttering, "I'm sorry!" again. As she pulled Jessie away, she could hear the lady behind her, telling everyone coming out of the store that little girls shouldn't be allowed to walk dogs they couldn't control.

"What happened?" said Maddie, as she came out of the store, clutching her magazine.

"Jessie stole that lady's cookies!"

Chloe whispered to her friend. "It was so embarrassing! I don't think I'll ever go in that store again!"

When they got home, Chloe carefully avoided telling Mom about their walk — except that Jessie had been good in the park. She went out into the yard and lay on the blanket under the apple tree in the shade. It was so hot.

Jessie lay down next to her, panting and wagging her tail as the bees buzzed past her nose.

Chloe reached out to pet her. "What am I going to do with you, Jessie?" she muttered. "Only two walks. One cut knee for me, one stolen cookie for you. This isn't working out very well, is it?"

Chapter Six

Grandpa came over the next day to look after Chloe while Mom and Dad went to the hospital, and as soon as they'd shut the front door behind them, Chloe pulled Grandpa over to the kitchen table to sit down and talk.

"What's the matter, Chlo?" Grandpa grinned at her. "You're looking very serious."

Chloe huffed out a sigh. "It is serious! I've tried everything, but Jessie can't stop getting into trouble. Mom's really angry with her, and I'm worried she might take her back to the dog breeder."

Grandpa looked down at Jessie, who was fighting with her stretchy rubber bone under the table. "I'm sure your mom wouldn't do that. She hasn't said anything to me. What's Jessie been doing?"

Chloe explained about the cereal, and the plants, and her knee, and then the stolen cookies. It did sound terrible when it was all in a long list, she realized.

Grandpa nodded slowly. "I didn't know she was so upset with Jessie, but I can see why…. It's been really hard for her and your dad, you know, worrying so much about Will. And they're worried about you, too, Chlo. Your mom thinks it's really spoiling your vacation."

"If I could get Jessie to behave well and go for walks without being afraid of what she might do, I'd be having a wonderful summer," Chloe replied.

"But you're already making a big difference," Grandpa pointed out, reaching across the table to cover her hand with his. "Think back to the day of Will's accident — just think about how you were with Jessie. I felt so sad, watching you. It looked like you secretly wanted to play with Jessie and Will, but you couldn't make yourself. And now look at you! I know the walks didn't turn out too well, but at least you went! And you haven't given up on Jessie, even after she's gotten you into trouble. I'm so proud of you."

Chloe turned pink and looked down at the table, feeling embarrassed. Dad had seen her cuddling Jessie the day before and told her it was great that she seemed to be getting along so well with the puppy, but no one had said it as nicely as that before.

"But it isn't making her any better behaved, Grandpa. I just don't know what to try next."

Grandpa hugged her. "Honestly, your mom won't send her back. But we don't want her getting any more stressed out than she is already." He nodded thoughtfully. "What that dog needs is a training class."

"Oh, yes!" Chloe bounced in her chair. "Will was going to take her, but he had football at the same time. He was planning to do it during summer vacation instead, but then we all forgot about it after the accident."

"How about it, then? You, Jessie, and me. Let's find ourselves a trainer. Come on, Chlo, show me some of those computer skills. Let's go and see what's going on around here."

Ten minutes later, Chloe and Grandpa had found a training class that was being held in the church hall around the corner. "Look, there's a class starting this Tuesday," Grandpa pointed out. "Perfect. Something fun for us to do while Maddie's away to keep you from feeling too sad about that horse camp."

"Can we call about the dog training now, Grandpa?" Chloe said eagerly. "I hope they aren't full."

Luckily, they weren't. Grandpa put down the phone, looking very pleased with himself.

"We can go?" Chloe asked eagerly. She was standing next to him, with Jessie dancing excitedly around her legs. Jessie could tell that something good was happening. Chloe sounded so happy.

Grandpa nodded. "And when I told Dan, the trainer, that Jessie was a Border Collie, he mentioned that he does agility sessions, too. So I've signed us up for a sample class in a few weeks."

"What's agility?" Chloe asked, stooping to hug Jessie and ruffling the fur around her neck. Jessie looked up at her adoringly.

"Haven't you ever seen it on TV?" Grandpa replied. "It's like horse show-jumping, but for dogs. Jessie isn't old enough for real agility classes yet, but he thought she'd enjoy the sample class."

Chloe beamed. "Jessie would love that."

"I'm sure she would. Dan said it's great for collies; it works off a lot of their energy. I thought it sounded like just what we need!"

Chloe was nervous about the first training class. What if Jessie didn't behave? It would be really embarrassing if she just wouldn't do as she was told. And Chloe was a tiny bit worried about all those other dogs, too. She wasn't scared of Jessie anymore, but she wasn't sure how she'd feel about a room full of dogs.

Luckily, there were only five in their class, and they were all puppies, too. Two Labradors, one black and one chocolate, a Cocker Spaniel, and one breed that Chloe didn't recognize. His owner said he was a mixed breed.

Jessie loved the class. Everyone said how beautiful she was, and Chloe kept telling her she was a good dog every time she did as she was told.

"She's doing really well." Dan, the trainer, crouched by Jessie and patted her gently. "Let's see you walk up the hall, turn at the end, and come back. Don't pull her, and walk slowly, okay? And give lots of praise."

Chloe looked down at Jessie lovingly. "Come on, Jessie, walk," she said, keeping her voice gentle but firm, like she'd been told.

Jessie showed off happily, trotting along right next to Chloe and turning perfectly, without Chloe having to pull her.

"Great. Give her one of your treats, Chloe. She's a natural." Dan looked really pleased.

"You are such a clever girl, Jessie!" Chloe said, holding out a dog biscuit.

Jessie gulped down the delicious meaty biscuit, wagging her tail happily. She loved dog training!

At the end of the class, Grandpa walked over. He'd been watching from the back of the hall, and Chloe had asked him to take some pictures to show Will when she went to visit him.

"We were so lucky that there was a course starting this week. Jessie seemed to really enjoy herself." Grandpa smiled. "I'm sure she'll love that agility sample class, too."

On their way home, Jessie walked close to Chloe, feeling happily tired after the class. She wanted to go home and curl up in her basket, and then later maybe Chloe would play those fun games with her in the yard.

There might even be more of the yummy treats.

Chloe's mom was thrilled that it had gone so well. "I'm going to have to come and watch one of these classes," she said. "It sounds like you and Jessie are doing great."

"We have beginners' training on Tuesdays and Thursdays for the next four weeks," Chloe explained.

"Are you coming with me to see Will?" Mom asked.

Chloe nodded excitedly. "Yes. I want to tell him how fantastic Jessie was at the class. He's going to be so proud of her! I didn't tell him we were going, just in case Jessie behaved really badly."

Will was watching a DVD on the TV above his bed, but he turned it off as soon as he saw Mom and Chloe. "Wow, it's good to see you," he said, grinning. "Mom, have they said how much longer I have to be in here?"

Mom shook her head. "I'm supposed to talk to Dr. Bedford today. Hopefully not much longer, now that you've started physical therapy."

Will made a face. "It's good being allowed to move, but I'm so slow! It's going to be forever before I can go for runs in the park with Jessie. How is she?"

Chloe beamed at him and pulled out her camera to show him the pictures that Grandpa had taken. "She's wonderful! Look!"

Will stared at them, frowning. "You

took her to dog training? But I was going to do that!"

Chloe looked at him in surprise. She had thought he'd be pleased. "I know, but—"

"I was really looking forward to it!" Will huffed. "She's my dog!"

"Actually, Will, she's a family dog," Mom said gently. "I know you've spent the most time with her, but Chloe's been taking care of her really well. You'll be able to go to the classes, too, when you're better."

But Will was still scowling, and he hardly spoke to Chloe for the rest of the visit.

Chapter Seven

When Jessie sneaked into Chloe's
room that night, she could feel that
something wasn't right. Ever since
Chloe had come home, she'd been so
quiet. She'd petted Jessie and played
with her, but she hadn't been quite the
same.

Jessie stood by Chloe's bed and looked
up hopefully.

"Hello, Jessie!" Chloe smiled and patted the comforter. "Come on! Up!"

Jessie bounced onto the bed and settled herself on Chloe's tummy, staring into her face. "Oof, you're heavy," Chloe said. "It's nice, though. You're like the best kind of teddy bear." She sighed.

Jessie put her head to one side and whined questioningly. What was wrong?

"I know you don't really understand, but you're a very good listener," Chloe said, tickling her under the chin.

Jessie wagged her tail sleepily and closed her eyes. She was still listening, but she was worn out after all that hard work at the class.

"I hadn't really thought about it until we went to the hospital tonight," Chloe said, gazing at the ceiling.

"Of course I'm still looking forward to Will coming home, but it's going to be hard when he comes back, too."

Jessie flicked one ear thoughtfully as Chloe mentioned Will.

"I know Mom said you're a family dog, but really you've always been mostly his. You're not going to want to play with me once you've got Will back...."

Chloe sighed and looked down at Jessie again. "I'm not even sure we can keep going to dog training. Will was so upset...." Then she smiled, a little sadly. Jessie was fast asleep, floppy as a rag doll, stretched out on her tummy.

"I'll make the most of my time with you while I can," she whispered, petting Jessie lovingly.

Grandpa was very firm with Chloe when she suggested giving up the dog-training classes until Will could take Jessie instead.

"No. Absolutely not, Chlo. That's not fair to you or Jessie. You saw how much she loved training, and she needs it, too. She was getting into bad habits. It's sad for Will, but he loves Jessie, and he'll understand. There'll be plenty more classes that he can take her to. I'm going to see him this afternoon, so I'll have a talk with him."

Chloe hugged him with relief. She really didn't want to give up the classes — that first one had been so much fun.

When she next went to see Will, he

glared at her as she came up to his bed, and she wondered if he was still angry.

"Grandpa says I have to say sorry," Will muttered grumpily. "He says I should be grateful to you for taking care of Jessie so well." He sighed. "And I am. It's just that I was really looking forward to the classes. But Jessie needs training now. I know it's not fair to make her wait."

Chloe beamed at him. "You'll be out of here soon, then you can take her. She's really good," she added.

It was true. They'd had quite a few classes now, as they were twice a week, and Jessie was a star at every one. There was going to be a competition at the final training session, Dan had said, and Chloe really wanted Jessie to do well.

They'd been practicing a lot in the yard. She didn't mention training to Will again, though; it didn't seem very fair.

She just wished Will could have come to the special agility sample class, too. As she and Grandpa watched Dan set up the course, she knew he would have loved it.

Dan had brought his two adult Border Collies to show everyone what to do. "Aren't they beautiful?" Chloe whispered to Jessie. "You're going to look like that when you're bigger."

Jessie wasn't really listening. She was staring eagerly at Dan as he took one of the collies, Marlo, to the start of the course. It had been set up in a big field on a nearby farm.

Jessie's tail was twitching with excitement and her eyes sparkled as she watched Marlo set off, speeding around the course, leaping over the jumps, darting in and out of the weaving poles, and shooting through a long pop-up tunnel. He even jumped through a hoop, and then finished by running up a seesaw and tipping it down. Everyone clapped when he and Dan completed the course, and Marlo just shook his ears proudly, as if to say it was nothing.

Dan and another instructor then began to demonstrate how to use the different equipment. Chloe and Jessie started with low jumps. Even though Jessie was tiny compared to some of the other dogs, she flew over the jumps easily.

Dan watched her, laughing. "Chloe, promise me that when Jessie is a year old and can go to the agility classes, you'll sign her up."

"Oh, she has to be a year old?" Chloe asked disappointedly.

Dan nodded. "Some of the agility equipment isn't suitable for puppies because they're still growing. Things like the weaving poles — those sticks that Marlo was going in and out of —

can hurt a young dog's back."

Chloe nodded. "I think she'd love to go to a class once she's old enough."

"Agility is great for collies; they're so bright and energetic. And it uses up all that energy, too. They can be a real handful when they're bored."

Chloe nodded. "Jessie was being so naughty before we came to training," she agreed. "She was a nightmare."

"You should definitely bring her to agility. Did you know some agility teachers run ABC classes?" Dan asked her, grinning. "Anything But Collies. Because they're so good at it, they leave all the other dogs in the dust!"

When they got back, Mom dashed out to meet them and hugged Chloe delightedly. "Will's coming home tomorrow! Isn't that wonderful?"

Chloe hugged her back. She had missed Will so much. Although it did hurt a little bit to see Jessie jumping up and down, wagging her whole back end, not just her tail, because she was so excited. "You're going to be so glad to see him, aren't you?" Chloe said, giving her a pet. "Will's hardly going to recognize you, now that your fur's so long!"

After dinner, Chloe spread herself out on the living room floor and taped together six big sheets of drawing paper.

"There you are! What are you doing?" Dad asked, peering around the living room door.

"Making a 'Welcome Home!' banner for Will. I thought I'd put it in the hallway. Can I tie it to the banisters?"

"Of course you can. That's a really nice idea, Chlo. Do you need any help?"

Chloe shook her head. "Only with the tying. Thanks, Dad."

The banner took a while, outlining the letters, then painting them with lots of different colors. When she'd finished filling in "Welcome Home!," Chloe decided to take a break and get some juice while the paint dried.

She came back with her drink and stood at the door to admire her work — which was now decorated with a pattern of blue and red paw prints.

"Jessie!" Chloe wailed. "You walked on it!"

Jessie looked up at her guiltily, and wagged her tail apologetically. Chloe laughed. "Actually, I bet Will would like it better like this, anyway." She smiled to herself, imagining how furious she would have been if Jessie had done something like that a few weeks ago. "You just want to welcome him back, too, don't you? We'd better wash your paws, though, before you track paint everywhere."

Jessie and Chloe sat on the window seat, staring out at the street, waiting for Will to come home. Jessie kept jumping down, running over to the front door, and then dashing back again. She was so excited her tail couldn't stop wagging. Will! Chloe had said Will was coming home!

Chloe peered out the window. "Yes! There's the car, Jessie. They're here!"

Jessie shot out into the hallway, barking excitedly and scratching at the door.

Chloe opened it, and they stood watching as Will struggled out of the car on his crutches.

Jessie looked up at Chloe uncertainly as she saw Will hobbling toward them, but Chloe smiled and shooed her forward. Will was beaming, and calling to  her, so she went to sniff him, and then licked his hands lovingly. She could tell that she shouldn't jump up.

"Good girl, Jessie," Mom said gratefully. "I was worried that she might be a little rough."

Will loved the banner. "Great painting, Jessie." He chuckled, balancing on one crutch to ruffle her fur. He looked up at Chloe. "Thanks for taking care of her. She looks great."

Chloe smiled proudly, but he was saying it as if she didn't have to worry anymore. It felt like Will was taking Jessie back now. She lagged behind as they went into the house. Feeling as though she should let Will and Jessie be on their own, she lingered in the hallway. She missed Jessie already!

Jessie led Will into the living room and lay down determinedly on his lap as soon as he sat down on the sofa.

"She's not letting you go again," Dad said, laughing.

Jessie sighed happily. But then she looked around for Chloe. Why wasn't she here, too?

Jessie sat up and licked Will's hand, then headed out into the hallway, where Chloe was sitting on the stairs. Jessie looked up at her and gave a worried little whine. Why was Chloe by herself? She took the hem of Chloe's dress in her teeth and tugged, very gently.

Chloe smiled at her, her eyes widening with hope. "You want me to come, too?" she whispered, and Jessie wagged her tail. Chloe leaned forward and kissed the top of her head. "You belong to both of us, now, don't you?" she whispered gratefully.

Chapter Eight

"Jessie! Jessie!" Chloe ran down the stairs, a worried edge creeping into her voice. She couldn't find Jessie anywhere. Or Will. But she had a horrible feeling that she knew where they were.

Will had hated being stuck in the house during the last few days. Almost more than he'd hated the hospital. He couldn't ride his bike or skateboard, and even if he wanted to go upstairs, Mom or Dad had to help. But not being able to walk Jessie was the worst thing of all. He was desperate to take her out. Mom had driven Chloe and him to the park the day after Will came home so that he could watch Jessie running around. But poor Jessie hadn't understood, and she'd kept coming back to Will and staring at him hopefully, wanting him to join in.

Ever since then, Will had been aching to take Jessie out to the park by himself.

"She's really well-behaved now, Mom," he'd pleaded that morning at breakfast. "It isn't far. Now that she's been to dog-training classes, I could take her, no problem."

"Of course you can't!" Mom sounded horrified. "You just got out of the hospital! You need to use your crutches; how can you possibly manage Jessie as well?"

But Chloe didn't think Will had been convinced. He'd just scowled into his cereal.

Chloe stopped short at the bottom of the stairs, her eyes wide. Will's crutches were propped up by the front door, and Jessie's leash was gone from its hook.

He'd taken her out, Chloe realized, nibbling her thumbnail anxiously. He'd gotten so irritable with everyone making a big deal over him that he'd decided to show them, and he'd taken Jessie for a walk on his own.

Chloe stared at the door. If she told,

Mom would have a fit. Better just to go and find them. She reached for the house keys and let herself quietly out of the house.

Jessie was walking beautifully, not pulling at all, just like she'd learned at the training classes. But Will was holding her leash strangely, she thought, looking up at him. He kept wobbling. He looked like he wanted to turn back, and they were only halfway to the park. Jessie stared up at him and whimpered. Something was wrong.

Will suddenly sat down on someone's front wall, gasping. "I'm sorry, Jessie," he muttered. "I shouldn't have brought you out; it was a silly idea, and now we're stuck."

Jessie pulled gently at the leash in his hand, but he tightened his grip. "No, I'm sorry, Jessie. We're not going to the park."

Jessie whined — she had to make him understand. If he let her go, she could get help! She took the leash in her teeth this time and tugged at it harder. Then she walked a couple of steps back in the direction of the house and barked encouragingly at him.

"No, I can't," Will tried to explain. "Oh! *You* want to go home? Do you know the way?" he asked doubtfully.

Home! Jessie sat down, wagging her tail. She pulled the leash with her teeth again, and this time he let it go.

"Go home, Jessie. Find Chloe," Will told her. The puppy licked his hand reassuringly before trotting off down the road as fast as she could. She felt anxious — she didn't like running along with her leash trailing like this. But she had to help Will.

Chloe dashed down their street, heading for the park. She really hoped Will hadn't done anything to make his leg worse. What if he'd fallen?

Suddenly, she spotted Jessie running toward her — on her own. Where was Will?

Jessie gave a delighted bark. She'd found Chloe! She jumped up at her, barking again and again, and Chloe hugged her tightly. "Good girl, Jessie. Shhh! Where's Will? Can you show me?" she asked, holding Jessie's front paws.

Jessie jumped down immediately and turned back, waiting for Chloe to pick up her leash. Then they raced along the road together.

Will was still sitting on the porch step when Jessie proudly led Chloe back to him. He was looking very white, and Chloe sat down next to him, wondering if he'd let her give him a hug. She compromised by putting an arm around his shoulder.

"Don't say it," he muttered.

"I didn't!"

Will smiled at her for a second. "I'm sorry. I should have listened to Mom. It's a good thing Jessie was here. She knew what to do — she made me let go of the leash so she could get you."

"She's terrific," Chloe told him, watching Jessie panting contently. "You should come to her training classes, you know. The last beginners' class is on Thursday. It's a special competition lesson. You'd be really proud of her." She stood up and helped him pull himself to his feet. Then they set off slowly down the road.

"Um, maybe," Will said quietly. "I'm sorry I was so jealous before. It's just that I was looking forward to taking her."

"You could help me practice with her," Chloe suggested. "Even if the walking parts are difficult, you could do sit and stay. And she needs to learn to behave correctly for you, too."

"I suppose so." Will looked a little more cheerful. "Grandpa told me about her stealing those cookies. They should have a cookie hunt in this competition. Jessie would win, wouldn't you?"

Jessie barked, ears pricked, and Will burst out laughing.

"I'm never taking her anywhere near a store ever again." Chloe shuddered. "Come on. If we're quick, Mom might not have noticed we've been gone."

They limped back home, with Jessie walking at a snail's pace beside them, giving them both loving looks.

"I can't believe how good she is!" Will told Chloe as he watched Jessie sitting on her own in the middle of the church hall, with a dog biscuit between her front paws.

"She isn't even looking at it!"

"She knows she'll get it in a minute," Chloe said, but she couldn't keep the proud smile off her face. "All that practice we've done has really helped."

Dan nodded at Chloe, and she walked back to Jessie. "Good girl!" Chloe said. "You can eat it now."

Jessie gulped down the treat happily. She could see Will grinning at her, too.

Dan wrote something on the piece of paper he was holding and looked around the room. "Great job, everyone! That's the end of the competition, so can you all line up along here with your dogs, please, and I'll announce the winners."

Chloe grabbed Will's arm and helped him to the center of the hall so that he could line up with Jessie, too. "She's your dog, too," she hissed, as he gave her an *I shouldn't be doing this!* look. "Intermediate training classes start next week, and I've told Dan we're both coming — we can take turns leashing her. You can be off your crutches for an hour by then, can't you?"

Will nodded, grinning. "I'm sure I'll manage."

Dan was walking along the line with a handful of shiny medals. "Well, it's been very tight, but we have a winner. Chloe and Will, can you bring Jessie out for her first-place medal, please!"

"Jessie, you won!" Chloe hugged her, quickly rubbing her cheek against Jessie's silky fur. "Come on, Will!"

As they made their way to the front, Chloe looked around delightedly at Mom and Dad and Grandpa, all clapping. Grandpa had the camera ready, too.

Dan handed Chloe the medal, and she bent down to pin it to Jessie's collar. The puppy looked up at Will on one side and Chloe on the other, both smiling. And she thumped her tail happily on the floor.

HOLLY WEBB

Holly Webb started out as a children's book editor, and wrote her first series for the publisher she worked for. She has been writing ever since, with more than 90 books to her name. Holly lives in England with her husband and three young sons. She has three pet cats, who are always nosing around when Holly is trying to type on her laptop.

For more information
about Holly Webb visit:

www.holly-webb.com
www.tigertalesbooks.com